Seeing Orange

Sara Cassidy

ILLUSTRATED BY
Amy Meissner

ORCA BOOK PUBLISHERS

Library and Archives Canada Cataloguing in Publication

Cassidy, Sara
Seeing orange / Sara Cassidy ; illustrated by Amy Meissner.
(Orca echoes)

Issued also in electronic formats.
ISBN 978-1-55469-991-9

I. Meissner, Amy II. Title. III. Series: Orca echoes
PS8555.A7812S43 2012   jc813'.54   C2012-902833-9

First published in the United States, 2012
Library of Congress Control Number: 2012938344

Summary: When a neighbor encourages Leland's artistic talents,
he finds the confidence to express his feelings to his grade two teacher.

Orca Book Publishers gratefully acknowledges the support for its publishing programs
provided by the following agencies: the Government of Canada through the Canada Book
Fund and the Canada Council for the Arts, and the Province of British Columbia
through the BC Arts Council and the Book Publishing Tax Credit.

*Orca Book Publishers is dedicated to preserving the environment and has printed
this book on Forest Stewardship Council® certified paper.*

Cover artwork and interior illustrations by Amy Meissner
Author photo by Amaya Tarasoff

ORCA BOOK PUBLISHERS
PO Box 5626, Stn. B
Victoria, BC Canada
V8R 6S4

ORCA BOOK PUBLISHERS
PO Box 468
Custer, WA USA
98240-0468

www.orcabook.com
Printed and bound in Canada.

15 14 13 12 • 4 3 2 1

~~~~~~~~~~~~~~~~~~~~~~~~~~~~~~~~

Author's Note

An artist named Justin Beckett said, "I could paint these mountains the way they look, but that isn't how I see them. Artists don't paint what things look like. They paint what they see."

Chapter One

Pumpkin is stretched out asleep in my pajama drawer. Now my pajamas will have her golden-orange hairs all over them.

Mom is reading on the front steps, a mug of smelly tea by her knee. She calls it *herbal* tea. But I call it *horrible* tea.

My sister Liza is singing in the bathtub. It's some song about setting fire to the rain. Liza only takes baths so she can sing in the bathroom. She likes the echoes. She calls them *acoustics*.

Silas is building LEGO spaceships on the floor of our frog-green bedroom. Later, he'll head outside to throw a tennis ball against the wall. Once, his ball went through the open bathroom window while Liza was in there singing. *Splash!* Did Liza ever scream!

And me? I'm under the piano bench. I've draped a blanket over it to make a secret cave. It's getting pretty hot in here. Maybe I'll go lie on the floor in the narrow space between Mom's bed and the wall. I could pretend I'm a luger speeding down an ice track. That'll cool me down.

I like the laundry room best. It's a scrubbed place. The air smells like soap. I like the white walls and the soft towers of clean, folded laundry. The only problem is the dirty laundry piled on the cement floor. It's like a stinky sleeping beast. If I look too long, it starts to breathe.

This morning, I drew a picture of Mom's sweater on the clothesline. The crayon that matched it was called persimmon. Apricot was too light. It was hard to draw the sweater's wrinkles. But I did a good job with the right sleeve that hung down as if it was reaching for something.

The kitchen is the busy room in our house. It's where we talk and play Scrabble. Silas doesn't usually sit for long. He wheels around and around the house on his Rollerblades. He only changes direction if he gets dizzy. "He'll damage the floors," visitors warn. Mom just shakes her head. "Having fun is more important than smooth floors," she says.

Some places in our house scare me. Like under the back porch. I only go there if we are playing hide-and-seek. I squat on top of the broken plant pots, hoping the pill bugs don't crawl over me. Old flower bouquets with brown petals and moldy stems rot in the dirt. Mom dumps vases out there when she can't get to the compost pile.

On school mornings, we jam up in our tiny front hallway. We cram our lunches into our schoolbags. Mom searches frantically for the car keys. Silas gulps down the last of his bowl of cereal. Liza pulls everything off the coat hooks to look for her favorite hoodie.

Move out of the way!

Where's my other shoe?

That's MY lunch.

Mom calls it the Hurry Flurry. These days, I don't like the Hurry Flurry. Because I don't want to go to school. My grade two teacher is Mr. Carling. No matter what I do, he's always mad at me.

Chapter Two

As soon as I enter the schoolyard, my heart starts to bang. It bangs like the big drum in the Victoria Day parade. My stomach feels like it's full of gravel. I can hardly walk. It's like I'm wading through high water. "Hurry up, Leland!" Liza hisses as she breezes past. But I don't hurry up. I freeze.

Delilah rescues me. Her shaggy belly presses against my thigh. I grab the square handle of her leather collar and let her lead me through the big front doors. She leads me down the shiny hallway into Mr. Carling's classroom. I hang up my jacket and change into my indoor shoes. Delilah snuggles into my cubby. She has to shrink a little to fit in there.

I once saw a dog like Delilah leading a woman down the street. The woman had long hair, freckles on her nose and strange white eyes that blinked a lot. Mom told me the woman didn't see well and the dog helped her get around. Delilah doesn't really help me *see*. She helps me *move*. Liza says Delilah is imaginary. She says I make her up. So what? She still helps me.

The carpet at the front of the classroom is the color of a rotting Christmas orange. But up close, it's amazing. It is made of a million, zillion tiny thread loops. Each loop is a single color: rust, copper, gold, bright orange. I like to stick the point of my pencil into a loop and pull until one end comes out. Sometimes the nib of my pencil breaks.

Mr. Carling shoves a piece of chalk into his chalk holder. He writes: *October 25*. The backs of his fingers are hairy. His hands are hairy too, and his arms. I wonder if his wrist is hairy under his watch strap. Maybe the strap hides a seam where he's stitched together, like a monster. I wonder if any of the other kids wear watches to hide their seams. Sam has one. He could be a—

"*Leland?*"

Mr. Carling looks at me hard. I look back at him, but it feels like there are miles between us. "Get your listening ears on," he says. "Where are the salmon spawning?"

"I don't know," I say.

"Goldstream River. We're going to see them on Thursday. There will be a permission form for your parents to sign…"

My grade one class went to Goldstream last year. I watched a giant maple leaf whistled down from a tree onto the back of a dead salmon that seagulls had been pecking at. The red leaf landed right on top of the salmon's red wound.

Everyone is standing and moving quickly to their desks. I hurry to mine. "What are we supposed to do?" I whisper to Angela.

"Write a story about the ocean," she says. "Duh!"

Angela's fire-orange hair is in a thick braid down her back. I asked her once if she was a Viking, but she didn't answer. Now, her hand scuttles across her page like a crab. I imagine streams of fire running through her, down her arm and out her hand. Her pencil marks are the ash.

"Let's see what you've done so far, Leland."

Mr. Carling is at my desk. I look at my page. It's blank. White as a bandage over someone's mouth.

"Nothing," Mr. Carling grunts. He shakes his head. "Nothing."

My stomach hurts. I stare at the bare page. It starts to blur and fall away. It falls down to the bottom of an ocean. Mr. Carling squats beside my desk. I smell the lemon drop that clicks against his teeth.

"You will have to stay in for recess," he says.

Delilah growls from the cubby. The bell rings. Everyone leaves except me and Mr. Carling.

I wipe tears from my eyes. The page floats up again. I write a title: *Raft*. I begin: *A Viking was alone on a raft. His salty tears landed in the salty ocean.* I trace over the *o* in *ocean*. I make the *o* bigger and bigger. I draw little waves inside it, and a raft. I work hard on drawing the ropes and swirling knots that hold the raft together.

Then I look out the window. Kids crawl all over the playground. Their footprints in the sand look like little waves.

Mr. Carling gets up from his desk and looks at my paper. "Well, at least you wrote *something*. You can go outside."

I race to the jungle gym. But as soon as I make it to the top, the bell rings to go back inside. I get one big jump for the whole recess. I dig my heels in deep, all the way down to where the sand is dark brown.

Chapter Three

On Tuesdays and Wednesdays after school, I pull the Red Flyer wagon, heavy with newspapers, down our street. Silas runs door to door delivering them. Our cat Pumpkin sometimes follows for a block, then turns back. Today, though, she stays longer. Silas waves his arms at her. "Shoo. Go home."

There's a house on our paper route that Silas and I call Gloomy Rooms. The front steps sag. Moss bubbles up between the roof shingles. The grass is high, and the bushes are dark tangles. Silas rolls up the newspaper and throws it onto the crooked front porch from as far away as he can. For a while afterward, everything seems a little scary. Then Yellow House cheers me up.

The yard of Yellow House is filled with bird baths. The woman who lives there always calls out, "Thanks!" Today, she's in the yard, watering a small tree. She's wearing a big gray sweater, and her jeans are tucked into rubber boots. When she sees us, her face crinkles into a smile. She waves.

My mind goes *click*. She has one hand on the hose and her other hand is waving. It's as if she's pumping the air for the water that is running through the hose.

After supper, I ask Liza to pour paints from the big plastic jugs into the muffin tin. Then I paint a picture of the woman with her arms out, one waving, one watering. I like my painting. I look at it over and over.

* * *

At breakfast, Mom looks worried. "Pumpkin didn't come home last night," she says.

"Maybe she got lost," Silas says. "Or hurt."

"I hope she's just on a walkabout," Mom says.

"Yeah, cats do that," Liza says. "They wander off for a few days."

"Not Pumpkin," I say.

I'm so worried about Pumpkin, I forget about Mr. Carling and walk right into the school without Delilah's help.

Chapter Four

"Boys!" Our neighbor Mikel waves a shiny can at me and Silas. "Engine oil," he pants. "Your wheels squeak. Puts my teeth on edge."

He gets down on a knee and squeezes oil into the wagon's wheels. "There." He stands. "Might as well take my paper now." He reaches for a newspaper.

"Not that one!" I cry.

Silas laughs. "Why not *that* one, Leland?"

I put on a baby voice. "That one's special," I say, and pout.

It works. Silas rolls his eyes. "Whatever. Here, Mikel, take this one."

Outside Gloomy Rooms, while Silas delivers the newspaper, I feel like I'm sinking. The sky is the color of tin foil, and the clouds are like steel wool. The wind blows. Leaves scatter. They scratch along the sidewalk and street.

Hurry, Silas.

Finally, Silas is back. "I heard the old man," he says. "Whistling in there. It sounded happy and lonely at the same time."

Moments later, we're at Yellow House. "I want to deliver the paper today," I say.

Silas raises his eyebrows. "That isn't our deal."

"Just this house," I say.

"I'm not paying you any more than usual," Silas says.

"I don't want more money!" I tell him.

I grab the newspaper that Mikel nearly took, unlatch the maroon gate and hurry up the walk. Birds chatter in the bushes. A water fountain gurgles and chimes. I smell sap, wet dirt and flowers.

It feels like I'm in another world, where the air is thicker.

Hidden inside the newspaper is my drawing of the woman watering her tree and waving. I slide it out and tuck it into the woman's colorful mailbox. I leave the newspaper on her doormat, which says *Welcome!*

I walk back through the chattering yard and step onto the gray sidewalk. The world goes plain again: houses, grass, brown telephone poles.

Chapter Five

After supper on Thursday, Mom calls a family meeting.

"Pumpkin hasn't been home in three days," she says. "I called the SPCA. They haven't seen an orange tabby."

"We need a poster," Silas says. "You know: *Lost Cat. Reward.*"

"Good idea," Mom says. "We need a good photo. One that shows her swirly markings, and the bald patch by her back hip, and her nibbled ear."

"And her different colored eyes," Silas says. "One green, the other blue."

"And her cracked red collar," Liza says. "With the little tarnished bell."

21

"No photo will show all that stuff," Silas says.

"I could draw a picture," I say.

"Yes!" Mom says. "Excellent idea. I'll scan it into the computer and print copies."

"And the reward can be my old iPod cover," Liza says.

Mom sets me up at the kitchen table with paper, paints and photos of Pumpkin. It's fun getting the colors of her fur. I mix yellow and red to make orange, and add white and black for different shades. I draw black stripes on her face and the little patch of white on her chin. I use a tomato-soup red for the collar, and mix gold and orange for her bell.

It kind of feels like I'm writing a letter to her. Every stroke of my paintbrush whispers, *Come home.* I paint her sunning in a square of light on the kitchen floor.

"Marvelous!" Mom says, staring at the painting. "You captured her. *That* is Pumpkin!"

"I wish it *really* was," I say.

"She'll come home, Leland."

"When?" I ask.

But Mom doesn't answer. She starts putting the paints away.

"Time for bed, Sweets," she says after a while.

My heart drops. For once, Mom doesn't know what is going to happen.

Chapter Six

I take Pumpkin's food dish outside and make a line of kibbles from the front door, down the front stairs, along the sidewalk to the end of the block. Maybe Pumpkin will smell them and nibble them one by one right to the front door.

On the way to school, we put up posters. *Have you seen Pumpkin? Reward!* Our phone number is on them. It's raining a little. I hope Pumpkin isn't wet and shivering, wherever she is.

I want to hide under the piano bench until I hear Pumpkin pad into the house to drink from the fish tank. That's what she does! The goldfish get out of her way.

Pumpkin doesn't really *do* a lot. She sleeps most of the time. But she makes our house feel warm. Like a fire in a fireplace. Lions make the jungle a jungle. Pumpkin makes our house a home.

* * *

We're going to Goldstream Park today. First, though, we have to write a story about salmon.

I write my title: *Sammen*. I look out the window. Some of the fall leaves are salmon-colored, orangey pink. Salmon get their colors from eating krill, which are pink, and shrimp, which are orange. People can turn orange too, if they eat too many carrots.

Suddenly, I see orange everywhere: the playground slide, the rust on the flagpole, a seagull's webbed feet. I look around the classroom and spy orange letters, orange clothing and orange book covers. Just thinking about orange made my eyes find it.

"Sammen?" Mr. Carling takes a deep breath. "I spelled salmon for you on the blackboard. S-a-l-m-o-n."

My face goes numb. I hope I'm turning invisible.

"You had better get some work done, Leland, or you won't be going to Goldstream," Mr. Carling says. My throat tightens. Delilah walks over and lies at my feet. She thumps her tail against the floor. *Shhh.*

"Focus, Leland! Your classmates are almost finished."

I try hard. I write: *A bald eagle fishes a ~~sammen~~ salmon from a lagoon. She carries it in her beak and flies over a schoolyard.* The bell rings. Recess!

"Leland, you need to stay and finish your story."

I sit back down. I stare at the classroom walls. There are no pictures on them, just the letters of the alphabet and a math chart. The classroom air is like metal—hard and thin. It's the opposite of Yellow House. There, the air is like feathers.

If I could write better, I'd write: *The salmon wriggles to get free. The eagle can't hold it. The salmon falls*

from the sky and crash-lands in the schoolyard below. Kids crowd around as it flips and flops. Delilah the dog noses through the crowd and gently takes the salmon in her teeth. She runs all the way to the ocean with the salmon in her mouth. She drops the fish into the salty water and barks goodbye as the fish swims away.

"Well, Leland?" Mr. Carling says.

"My hand hurts," I say.

"How can it hurt? You've hardly written a thing."

I try not to cry.

"I write slow," I say. "Can I draw a picture?"

"Leland, you aren't in grade two to draw pictures," Mr. Carling says as he unwraps a candy. I would like a candy.

Sammen stink, I write.

The bell rings. The kids stomp in, big and loud and smelling like the wind.

Chapter Seven

Mr. Carling lets me go to Goldstream after all. It's a long, bumpy ride on the orange school bus. At the park, a biologist cuts open a dead salmon. She teaches us not to say *Yuck!* but rather, *How interesting!* The salmon's heart is a deep red-purple. Its liver is purple-brown. Its brain is white! The biologist tells us that a salmon's eye weighs more than its brain does! It makes me wonder if salmon think with their eyes. I sometimes feel that I do.

The biologist holds one of the fish's eyeballs between her thumb and finger, and we take turns looking through it. Everything is upside down!

The fish's brain turns everything right-side up again. The biologist says our brains do the same thing.

I go into the woods and lie down along the long trunk of a fallen tree. I stretch my head back so everything is upside down. I just lie there listening, watching the tree branches take root in the blue sky. I close my eyes. The moss and leaves smell good. Then I hear heavy footsteps.

I open my eyes. Mr. Carling is right beside me.

"Leland! Are you hurt?" He speaks quickly.

"I'm fine," I say.

"Thank goodness," Mr. Carling says. He wipes his forehead with his hand. Then he asks sharply, "Why are you off the trail?"

I spy a bright piece of garbage in the brush.

"My granola-bar wrapper blew away," I lie. "I was getting it. I...I tripped."

I get up. Mr. Carling brushes dirt and leaves from my jacket.

"We have to catch up to the others," he says, heading back to the trail. Then he falls.

"Ouch!" he yells. He stays on the ground, rubbing his foot. "Oh. Oh." He tries to stand and winces.

"Leland, I need you to hurry to the nature house," he says. He points through the woods, to a building with a red roof. "Tell Madame Maillot that I've twisted my ankle." Madame Maillot is a teacher that is helping him today. "Tell her I've gone to the bus." Mr. Carling gives me a serious look. "Don't get lost, Leland. Don't forget what you need to tell Madame Maillot."

I nod and hurry to the path. I look back once to see Mr. Carling hopping toward the bus. He stops to rest every few hops.

I chant:

Madame Maillot, Madame Maillot
Madame Maillot has got to know

I cross a little bridge. The stream below sounds like xylophone music. I crouch and peer through the slats of the bridge. The water under the bridge wrinkles and unwrinkles as it moves. It never stops. I drop a stick over the rail, then run to the other side and watch it pop out. The stick bobs along. It gets smaller and smaller until I can't see it anymore. I grab a handful of leaves and toss them down. They bounce along on the back of the stream, like little canoes. The stream burbles. I put my hand to my ear to listen. It says:

Madame Maillot, Madame Maillot

I forgot! I run like mad. In the nature house, Madame Maillot is talking to the class. I grab her sleeve. "Not now, Leland," she says.

But I say, "Yes, now. Mr. Carling fell in the forest. He twisted his ankle. He will wait for us on the bus."

"Thank you, Leland," Madame Maillot says. She gets down on her knee and looks me in the eye. "Well done," she says.

* * *

Mom doesn't usually answer the phone during supper, but tonight she jumps up when it rings.

She listens for a moment. "Yes! Great! Thank you!" she says. She hangs up and sighs. "That was no help. The caller saw Pumpkin on our street—five days ago."

We're quiet as we clear the table. Mom opens the window and shakes out the tablecloth, which she does every night. Then she hangs the tablecloth over the back of her chair, which is normally the sign for us to get into our pajamas. Then the phone rings again.

"Hello?" Mom says. "Yes. That's our poster. Oh. My son, Leland. Yes, quite an artist. He did what? The house with the bird baths?"

Mom gives me a funny look. "Leland, someone wants to talk to you."

I take the phone. "Hello?" I ask.

"Hello!" The woman's deep voice makes me think of chestnuts. "My name is Pamela."

"Camelot?"

"No, *Pamela*. I got your picture, Leland. In my mailbox."

"Oh, it's *you*!" I say.

"You didn't sign it. But I saw your poster. I hope you find your lost cat. I knew when I saw the poster that it was the same artist. You have a special way of mixing colors."

"Thank you," I say. Silas is Rollerblading around me, and Liza is practicing her fiddle. But all I really hear is Pamela's warm voice.

"I'm a painter too," she says. "Would you like to paint with me sometime?"

"When?" I'm so excited I nearly shout.

"How about tomorrow? After school."

"How about *instead* of school?" I ask.

Pamela laughs. "*After.*"

Chapter Eight

Mr. Carling is probably very mad at me. Delilah has to pull hard to get me to the classroom. Mr. Carling is on crutches. His left foot is in a pink-brown bandage.

"Is it broken?" Angela asks.

"It's only a sprain," Mr. Carling says.

I give him the card I made last night. I drew dozens of feet—human feet, webbed seagull feet, bald eagle claws, bear paws. And I wrote very carefully: *I hope your foot is strong again soon. Sorry. Leland.*

"Thank you, Leland," he says.

I can't tell if he's angry or not. He looks a little sad. He doesn't get mad at me all day. But it's raining, which means everyone has to stay in for recess.

* * *

After school, Mom walks me to Pamela's house. I've packed paintbrushes, paints and cookies in my backpack. Mom's best friend knows Pamela and told Mom I'd be safe with her. We open the gate to her yard, and it's like pushing a button: birds sing and the smells of grass and flowers swarm us.

Pamela bursts out the front door. She's wearing a long red skirt, a fuzzy olive-green hat and a thick white sweater with buttons made of pencil stubs.

"I hope you brought a sweater," she says. "I don't turn on the heat unless the pipes are going to freeze. The cold keeps me sharp!"

Inside, the walls are covered in paintings and drawings. The shelves and windowsills are filled with seashells, bird bones, stones and nests.

"Your mom paid for ten painting lessons," Pamela says. "But I'm sure you have as much to teach me as I have to teach you."

She leads me into a room with a bouncy-looking velvet couch and two easels in front of the fireplace.

"First we're going to wash the windows," Pamela says. She hands me a cloth and a spray bottle. "We can't paint without good light. Good light makes good shadows. Good shadows make good shapes."

After the windows are clean, Pamela suggests we paint pictures of the fireplace.

"With no fire?" I ask.

"Sure. When we look at a fireplace, all we see is the fire. What will we see if there's no fire?"

I peer into the fireplace. The ash is like feathers. I stand back and look at the chimney. The bricks are orange and red, just like fire.

"Artists don't paint what things *look* like. Artists paint what they *see*," Pamela says. "Just paint what you see, Leland."

So I paint a pile of feathers in the grate and dark-orange flames licking up around it. The fireplace, the mantelpiece and the chimney are fire!

"Wonderful!" Pamela exclaims.

Her painting is spooky. She painted every piece of blackened wood, every soot stain, every dirty crack in the bricks.

"Why did you paint it so sad?" I ask. "You seem so happy."

"I am happy," Pamela says. "But maybe I'm happy because I don't hide from sad things. I don't pretend they don't exist."

Chapter Nine

I have been thinking about what Pamela said about not being scared of sad things. I thought about the place under the back stairs with the broken pots. One day after school, I put on a sweater and drag a chair down the back stairs. I sit there with my notebook and drawing pencils and stare at the cobwebs and shriveled spiders. I feel frightened. But I take a deep breath. Nothing here can really hurt me.

As I draw, I see *why* the stuff is there. The spiders can spin webs, safe from rain. The pill bugs eat the rotting bouquets. I don't like the bits of plastic garbage though. They stand out too much. I color them superbright.

Liza opens her bedroom window and asks what on earth I am doing. A few minutes later she joins me.

"Here," she says.

"What are they?" I ask.

"Gloves."

"I can't draw with gloves on!"

"You're right," she says. She goes back into the house and returns a minute later.

"Now try them."

"Cool!" I say. She cut the fingers off the gloves! My hands are warm, but my fingers are free to hold the pencil.

Pamela taught me to draw as if the nib of the pencil was my eye. She said to follow the edges of things as if the pencil was my eye moving along them. It is difficult to draw the broken edges of the pots. They're so sharp, they hurt my eyes!

At our next class, I show Pamela my drawing. "What are the colored things?" she asks.

"Bits of plastic," I tell her. "That neon-orange thing is a Play-Doh lid. That's the handle of an old beach shovel, and that's the top from a peanut-butter jar. I don't like them."

"Why?"

"Because they don't move. They don't change. They just..." I can't find the right words.

"They stand out," Pamela says. "Plastic is stubborn. It's kind of selfish, isn't it? It doesn't really join the world."

"Yeah! That's what I feel!" I say.

"I know," Pamela says. "Your drawing showed me."

* * *

Mr. Carling moves between the desks on crutches. We're supposed to be writing about rain. Angela's hand moves across her page so quickly, it's as though her fingers *tell* the page her story. I write: *Rain knocks the last leaves from the trees. Puddles are mirrors.*

"You'll have to stay in for a while," Mr. Carling sighs when he sees my story.

I sigh too. But then Delilah growls, and I start to feel hot. My heart pounds in my head. I'm angry. Really angry. This must be what Mom calls *seeing red*. I can't see anything, just red air.

The recess bell rings, and everyone leaves except me. Mr. Carling stays at his desk. I look at him for a long time, the way I looked at the fireplace and the cobwebs under the stairs. I see him. He's like a little bird, half busy, half nervous.

"Are you mad at me because you hurt your foot?" I ask.

Mr. Carling looks up. He raises his eyebrows. "I *was*," he says. "But it was mostly my fault. I'm clumsy on rough ground."

"I like rough ground," I say.

"I like to stick to the path."

"I like it *off* the path," I say. "I love the woods. Almost as much as I love drawing—"

"And daydreaming?"

Delilah growls and bares her teeth.

"I don't daydream," I say. "I think about stuff."

"Listen, Leland. You're at school to learn," Mr. Carling says. "You have lots of time to play and daydream, or *think*, before and after school, all evening and all weekend. You only need to be on the path during the school day."

"On the path?" I ask.

"Focused. On your work."

"Mr. Carling?"

"Yes?"

I take a deep breath, like I did before I looked under the back stairs. "I don't like it when you keep me in at recess," I say. "It doesn't make me write faster. It just makes me sad."

"I see," Mr. Carling says. He bites his lip and looks at the ceiling. "I guess it's like me being stuck on crutches just because I'm a little clumsy," he finally says. "I've always been clumsy. Why should I be punished for it? You have a wandering mind. I know you're clever, Leland. And creative. I'm not that creative."

"Oh, you probably are," I say. "You just need to take some lessons, maybe."

"How about we make a deal?" Mr. Carling asks. "I'll be more patient."

"And I'll try harder to do my work," I say.

"If I see that you're trying, I won't keep you in."

Mr. Carling puts his hand out. I put my fist out. Mr. Carling closes his hand and knuckle-bumps me. Then Delilah unfolds herself from my cubby, shakes herself out and wanders right out of the room with a little bark. She is saying goodbye. She is telling me that I don't need her anymore.

"You can go out now, Leland," Mr. Carling says. I dash outside. I climb to the top of the jungle gym and jump off, making deep footprints in the sand, like brushstrokes on canvas.

Chapter Ten

Pamela and I are at our easels in front of different windows. We are to paint every single thing we see.

"Think of the window as a painting that we are copying," Pamela says. "Remember: look, watch, stare, peer, study, observe."

My window is filled with Mr. Gloomy Rooms's backyard. I paint the old rowboat lying upside down in long grass. I copy every slat of wood on his old garage. I'm working on the garage window when I see something move. Something orange. It's waving. It's a tail!

"Pumpkin!" I shout.

Pamela runs over, paintbrush in her hand. "Where?"

"In that garage!"

Pamela leaps into her rubber boots. I grab my sweatshirt. We run to Gloomy Rooms and peer into the garage. It's her! Pumpkin! She's so thin! She meows like a kitten. Pamela yanks on the shed door. It scrapes against the ground. Pumpkin jumps into my arms. She is bony and some of her fur has fallen out.

"What a cutie!" says Pamela.

"She's not usually so skinny," I say, crying. "Oh, Pumpkin!" I'm happy and sad at once.

"What is going on?" Mr. Gloomy Rooms is at the back door of his house. He's got a bristly beard and is wearing full-body long johns.

"This cat has been in your garage for a while, Geoffrey," Pamela says.

"Must have snuck in last week when I fetched a can of paint."

"Didn't you hear her meowing?" I ask.

"What did you say?" Mr. Gloomy Rooms shouts.

"Geoffrey doesn't hear too well," Pamela says.

"What's that?" Geoffrey asks.

"We should wrap her up," Pamela says.

"Yes! Good idea. Come in, come in."

We follow Mr. Gloomy Rooms—Geoffrey—into his house. It's dark inside but tidy. We sit at his kitchen table, which is turquoise and flecked with golden stars.

Geoffrey wraps a tea towel around Pumpkin, who purrs on my lap. Then he heats a pot of milk on the stove.

"Can I phone home?" I ask.

"I don't have a phone," Geoffrey says. He laughs when he sees how shocked I am. "I don't need one. I've got no kids or relatives to check on. I never married."

"Do you have email?" I ask.

Geoffrey laughs. "Lord, no!" He looks into my eyes as if he's looking for something deep inside.

"I'm eighty-six years old," he says. "I used to deliver coal, the same as you and your brother deliver newspapers."

He pours milk into a saucer. Pumpkin laps it up.

"Poor girl," Geoffrey says. "She'll be all right. Probably caught a few mice in there to keep her engine running. How did you know she was in there?"

"I was looking," I say, "really, really hard."

* * *

We eat a special supper to celebrate Pumpkin's return: sardines on toast. Pumpkin gets to eat at the table.

"So, does Leland get the reward?" Silas asks.

"I think Geoffrey should," Mom says.

"But he didn't do anything!" Liza says.

"No, but he feels really badly that he locked Pumpkin in, even if it was an accident," Mom says.

"He's doesn't need an iPod cover," I say. "He doesn't even have a phone."

"How about yard work?" Silas says. "His grass sure needs a trim. I could do that."

"I could weed," Liza says.

"I could borrow Mikel's oil can and oil the hinges on his gate," I say.

After supper, Mom shakes out the tablecloth, and Silas lets Pumpkin out the back door for her evening roam. "Don't go far," he warns her.

I sit at the dining-room table with my paints and brushes. I work on a picture of an old man wearing white long johns in a tidy kitchen, pouring warm milk into a dish for a golden-orange tabby cat. On the way to school tomorrow morning, I will tuck it under Old Geoffrey's door.

I will make sure my name is on it.

Sara Cassidy has worked as a youth hostel manager, a tree planter in five Canadian provinces and a newspaper reporter. Her poetry, fiction and articles have been widely published, and she has won a Gold National Magazine Award. She lives in Victoria, British Columbia, with her three children, a cat named Pumpkin and two goldfish. Leland also appears with his family in Sara's two novels in the Orca Currents series, *Slick* and *Windfall*. For more information, visit www.saracassidywriter.com.